P9-DDL-872

There Is a TRIBE of KIDS

LANE SMITH

Roaring Brook Press
New York

For Jane Enlow

Copyright © 2016 by Lane Smith
Published by Roaring Brook Press
Roaring Brook Press is a division of
Holtzbrinck Publishing Holdings Limited Partnership
175 Fifth Avenue, New York, New York 10010
mackids.com

Library of Congress Cataloging-in-Publication Data

Smith, Lane, author.
  There is a tribe of kids / Lane Smith. — First edition.
     pages cm
  Summary: Simple text follows a young boy and the many animals he meets
on his adventure through the jungle.
  ISBN 978-1-62672-056-5 (hardcover)
1. Animals—Nomenclature—Juvenile fiction. [1. Animals—Nomenclature—
Fiction.] I. Title.
  PZ7.S6538Th 2016
  [E]—dc23
                                        2015013771

Our books may be purchased in bulk for promotional, educational,
or business use. Please contact your local bookseller or the Macmillan
Corporate and Premium Sales Department at (800) 221-7945 ext. 5442 or
by e-mail at MacmillanSpecialMarkets@macmillan.com

The illustrations in this book were painted in oils and sprayed with an acrylic
varnish to create various mottled textures. Also used were colored pencils,
graphite, traditional cut and paste, and digital cut and paste.

First edition 2016
Book design by Molly Leach
Printed in China by RR Donnelley Asia Printing Solutions Ltd.,
Dongguan City, Guangdong Province

10 9 8 7 6 5 4 3 2 1

R0445254151

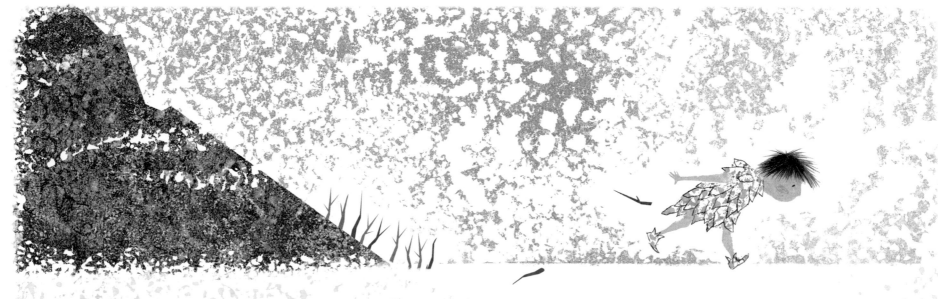

There was a TRIBE *of* KIDS.

There was a COLONY *of* PENGUINS.

There was a SMACK *of* JELLYFISH.

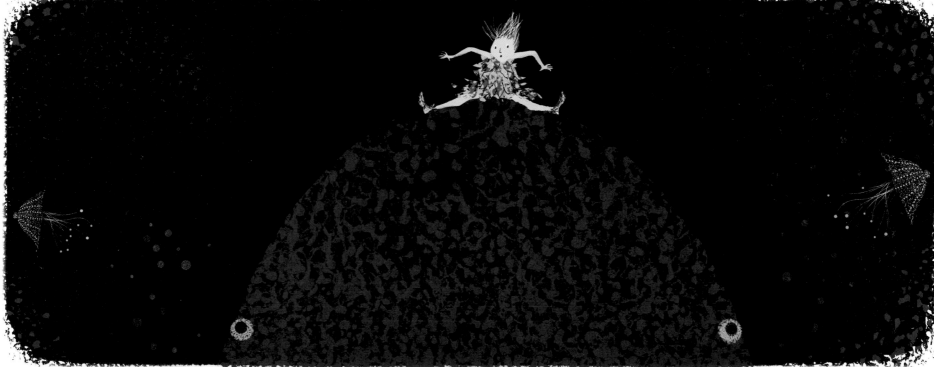

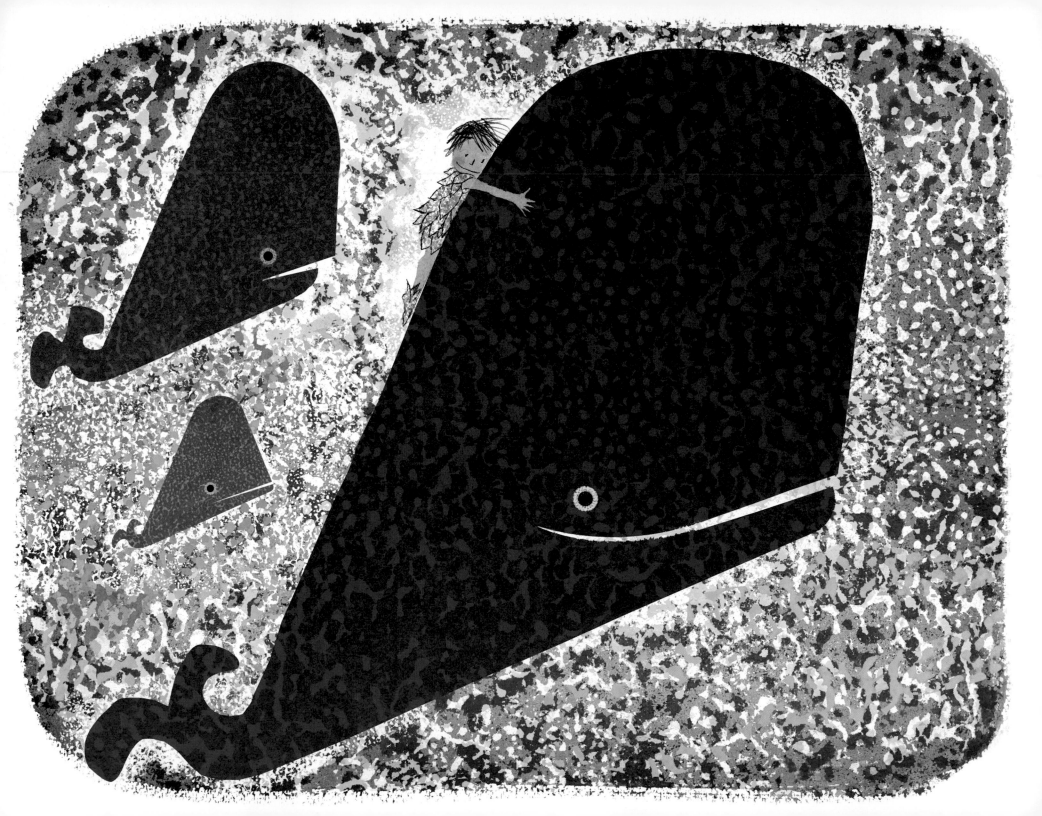

There was

a POD

of WHALES.

There was an
UNKINDNESS *of* RAVENS.

There was a FORMATION *of* ROCKS.

There was a

PILE *of* RUBBLE.

There was a GROWTH *of* PLANTS.

There was a

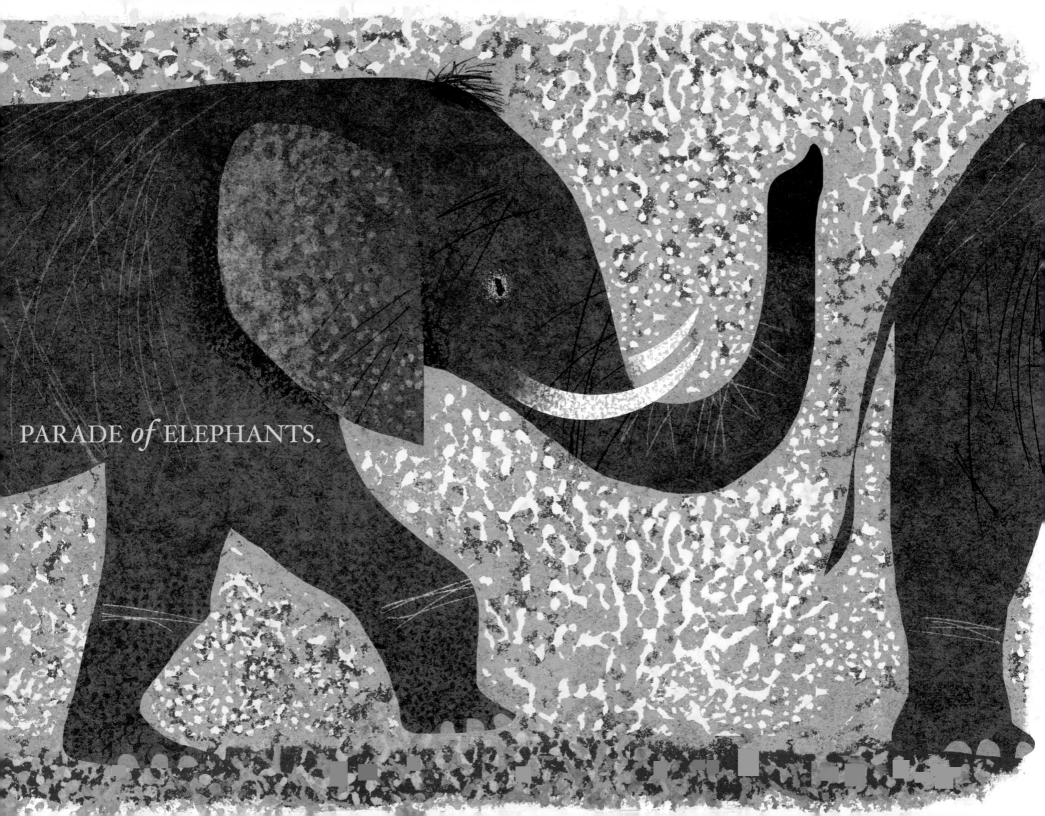

PARADE *of* ELEPHANTS.

There was a TROOP *of* MONKEYS.

There was a
CRASH *of* RHINOS.

There was a BAND *of* GORILLAS.

There was a TURN *of* TURTLES.

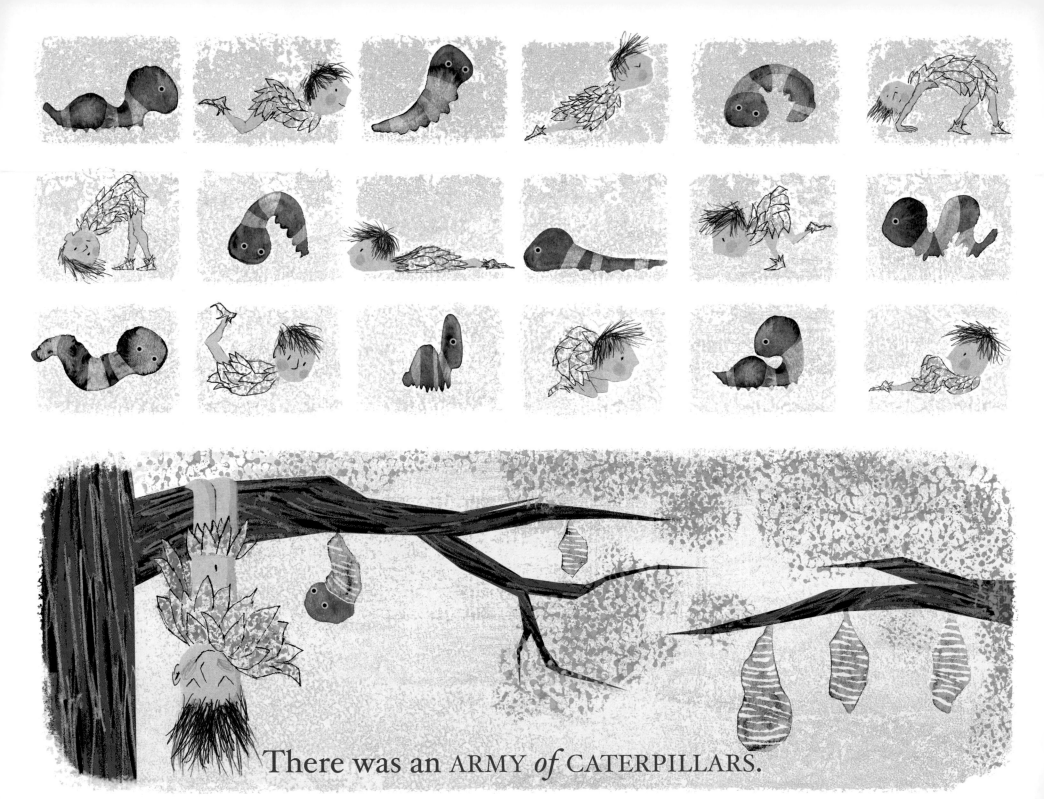

There was an ARMY *of* CATERPILLARS.

There was a FLIGHT
of BUTTERFLIES.

There was a SPRINKLE  *of* LIGHTNING BUGS.

There was a FAMILY *of* STARS.

There was an OCEAN *of* BLUE.

There was a
BED *of* CLAMS.

There was a NIGHT *of* DREAMS.

There was a
TRAIL *of* SHELLS.

There was . . .

a TRIBE *of* KIDS.

There is a

TRIBE of KIDS.